itch

Sheenginee B

PARTRIDGE

A Penguin Random House Company

To order additional copies of this book, contact
Partridge India
000 800 10062 62
www.partridgepublishing.com/india
orders.india@partridgepublishing.com

Contents

My first to my first,

dedicated to the memories of SAKU (2006–2009)

Preface

I love books—The crystal sparkling words, the fine lines on the pages . . . . And the gullibility. Especially, the gullibility. The moment you want to own any, they instantly become yours.

Fine Lies

I fool myself with metaphors. I tell myself stories of the other world. The perfect world. I lie.

Not too long ago, I met my kindred spirit. As we made wanton love, he told me how he had been looking for me all his life. He told me he loved me. He lied.

Lies are so sheer. We are full of them. They are full of us. We can never be without each other. We are made of each other.

Little Green Elf

In a fictitious parallel world, you would have been the little elf. Not the typical waif-like elf, however. You would have shiny oily eyes and a stocky body draped in an evil green cloak. The hair combed back while you chuckled and rubbed your palms together. Even in the real world, you chuckled demonically, quiet and rumbling like a vicious thunderstorm. Just the way chuckles should be. Define chuckle?

I often suffer from what I call, 'the midnight paranoia' where I wake up with a start, to my body breaking into pins and needles. I blame the coldness. That is the good thing about the head; one diffused smoky idea victimized for atrophy and it retains that idea, vestigial as it might be. So, it is the cold.

After one such breakout, as I try to sleep, I suddenly feel one of your legs intertwining with mine. The way it used to. I have always found, legs wrapping around legs, a very delicate experience, where endearments are uttered without a vocabulary.

Do you still find me strange?

I attack the thought furiously and keep my eyes closed. Since you refused to take us to our higher ground, I have been attacking everything. This and that. Those and them. Frail arms do flap.

But your leg keeps snaking up. I have to open my eyes now. Snakes in bed are dangerous.

I wonder if delusions should always be cruel.

I am going to have to find myself a reason to sleep any further.

The Man and the Machine

There is a man at the corner of the road whenever I take the bus. He wears the same blue jacket and follows me with his eyes. In my mind, I ask him, 'Are you the one?'

I never break myself gently.

*   *   *

What is coping? Denial or defence? Defence and Denial. Only denial. Only defence. I stare at the possibilities and choose none. Coping is nothing but flinging yourself at the dirt, getting moist and eventually caked, megalomania and grazing rock bottom long enough for it to feel like your own.

Like, right now I am a monomaniac. Right now, it is only about pain. Sick, stupid pain that reeks of stupidity. It is not even intelligible enough to be someone's joke. Like those funny horror movies where kids laugh when the blonde protagonist gets disembowelled. Blonde guts on the floor and laughter.

My form of coping is to bury myself. Duck my head into anonymity, where I do not stand out as a separate colour but be an overlooked tint in a mottled tapestry. Like, losing yourself in a crowd. I like the strangeness of strangers, the familiarity of strangers. How defaced they are, how similar they are. From the way they talk, you will really believe that they have seen everything. The innocence is refreshing, like a very cold shower in a hot, sultry afternoon.

For just a moment, you live each of their lives. Be them. Crawl into their bodies, melt and not exist as yourself. This is such beautiful cleansing, even delirious. I like delirium.

Right now, I choose to be this very senile lady with a polka dotted shopping bag. Her frizzy white hair glistens like fine silk from where I look. Her moves are measured, just the way it is when we first learn to walk. Such children they are. Her wrinkled face is untiringly smiling as if she is able to hear some incredible inconspicuous music that no one else can.

Why I choose to be her?

Her right arm is snugly tucked under a gentleman's left, which I take to be her grandson. He walks as slowly so as not to disrupt her pace, lightly manoeuvring, like a kind shepherd. I need that unadulterated affection.

In my dreams at night I hear your voice bellow:

'You take too much'

I give too much too.

The Hangover

The mornings are always repeating themselves. They are used to circling around the same circle. They are improperly monotonous. The streets are empty and poised, belying the violence that runs underneath. Violence in the ducts, violence in the veins. The clock shows 5.12 am. This darkness of the morning has no golden haze; it is a weapon; a sling blade, a hammer, a scythe.

Why I chose to be a writer is beyond me. Or maybe not. But love for words is not a sufficient reason. Then, what else could I have done? I am guilty of lacking too much talent. The things I write are half-hearted attempts to earn a living. I pay my bills and I am happy. Mediocrity suits me. It is comfortable and laidback. Ambition is scary.

One swig of the murky coffee; there is nothing like lukewarm bitter coffee. How I hate mornings and their distasteful aftertastes. Reminds me of *bazaars* when I was a kid. To elucidate, a disgruntled kid and an ordinary father. His hands sternly wrenching me away from the sad canals of fishy blood, silvery scales, chunks of skinned meat; away from butchers, money making and loss. But he did a bad job of it, because my shoes were always dirty when I got back home and there would always be one splotch of that tabooed pulp somewhere on my dress.

Back in my household, we always had tea. Coffee was considered too *shahebi*, or differently said, unaffordable. My mother always put too much sugar in the tea, but I never said so. I was only allowed a few sips when she was happy and was feeling queerly magnanimous.

*   *   *

My city is the smog city of dilution; diluted people, words, sleep, sloth, sugar, mud. Soggy and interlaced, there seems to be an unrecognizable granulated terrain passing through them all. All connected like dots on a map. It is more tenuous than it looks; this dotty passage is everything but it does not know that. It thinks it does not matter, often that it does not even exist. Self-delusion has never been more vibrant, climaxing like a wild child making love for the first time.

Through this portal of dubious self assertion, my mother lives alone in a one bedroom flat in *Southern Avenue*. One dot on the map. I stay a few miles away in another dot called *Jadavpur*. My mother is essentially a mother. A little skewed but that is alright. She is convinced that I am a closet genius. Her conviction in such appalling times is heart-warming, though slightly late.

We have dinner together once a week, where she prattles on happily and I keep nodding. I nod well. But often, she stops midway and asks for an opinion, which necessitates immediate focus. If I stutter, she lashes out at me for being inconsiderate. May be I am, but I am considerate enough to never argue. When push comes to shove, I am an efficient escapist. For somebody who loved confrontations, I learnt this lesson the hard way. The very hard way.

Since I moved out two years ago, this weekly, (usually) Saturday dinner tradition has been maintained. I actually bother to take out the best dishes, get a bottle of wine, chop vegetables in frenzy and cook. Generally it is me eating out of a bowl or lazily feeding on leftover pizzas. Cold pizzas make you burp and are good for flaking, lightly wound souls.

Tonight, she asks about you and I immediately break out in cold sweat. This is what a heart attack must feel like. The meat in my mouth turns to saw dust, all my culinary efforts in vain. Nevertheless, I glibly tell her something and surprisingly the obscurity satisfies her. I am a good pretender, like you.

Post-dinner, I drive her back home in my nondescript little car. While bidding goodbye she says she cannot wait to see me again. Mothers are such splendid creatures, only when old though.

On my way back, I think I see someone familiar. I stop to look but traces of that somebody is gone. For a hopeful moment, I think it is you; being my midnight stalker, plaintively beating down dust, murdering me in your head, fornicating in heightened cruelty.

*   *   *

The inky blackness of the night makes the past swirl, beyond my body. It is a shape shifter and does what it likes and I suddenly hear you say 'You know what, we laugh a lot together. That is a good thing'

The near empty wine bottle stares at me blankly. The first time I ever had red wine was with you. Four glasses down and I had suddenly flung myself on the table weeping over the memory of somebody hurting me in the past. Your black t-shirt I had wept on while you patted my hair. That night you kissed my palm for the first time and I felt your lips. Do you remember?

*   *   *

We have had the greatest love when we were most oblivious.

Respite

My best friend T is an insomniac. That is how we became friends, so maybe that is a good thing for us. That is how we became friends, is because I refused to talk to her during the day. At least that is what she claims. I am ambivalent about our beginnings but she is in my life now. She is married to a great man who she does not love. He accepts that and subverts morally incongruent young adults freely. I must mention he is bald and has charm.

My friend counters this composed infidelity with loose talk (which includes telling a mutual friend once 'Do you know your husband grabbed my tits at the Christmas party last year?' during a drunken stupor, binge drinking (with chain smoking) and retrogressive analysis slash advices. Post my apocalypse, she has been on an apocalyptic high. She slurs on phone indefinitely, blows smoke in my face through the phone, describes how cunnilingus should be, that old fashioned sex is greasy and finally always ending emphatically with that I am a misunderstood moron. Let me explain, that I am really a moron but people do not understand that.

Her growing euphoria at my sad denouement is something I thoroughly enjoy. The only thing I enjoy. There is nothing worse than pity for a poor lover. Conforming to social standards of consolation will never be her style, so she kicks me in the gut. She is my 2009 Tyler Durden, un-imaginary but curiously similar ten-year-later copy. She chemically burns me with her sliced, depraved victory. I can see her, in flimsy negligee, thin cigarettes between her thin lips, coy and volatile, the creative detonator. She wants to incinerate my door down and burn my only living bed, but I keep her limited to radio signals.

However, I am a tougher unnamed Narrator. I do not sob and denounce relationships. I do not call men pigs. I do not want to. I reject her as my purgatory.

So she says,

'You are hardly working'

There. I swallow down a mouthful of flaming saliva and smile. I cannot say I am not proud of myself.

'Do you think I don' t understand?'

I know that beyond the compost waste, her heart is beating somewhere—a regenerative heart sprouting hands and feet, tiny strands of muscles.

'Do you need me to give you a glass of water?' I ask. 'You might need that to douse your burning chaos'

She snaps and winds up tightly. I hear the flicker of her lighter and her harsh exhale.

'Take my smoke palace'

I feel something welling up inside me. There is going to be a war soon.

*   *   *

Hands thrust into my pockets, I make my way to the supermarket; T' s inhalations and exhalations, her smoky unreality I leave behind. This is a different supermarket, more busy and bustling. It is a crazy hullabaloo of green vegetables, often also red, yellow and purple; people with thinning hair, flaky scalps, conjoined memories, sonorous laughter. I am just another automaton.

My hands seize things in a blur; scented blur kisses my eyes. Chores are my crackling pandemonium of the day. Like rinsing old rags of cloths can have a lot of objectivity. It has to be dipped into the right amount of water, wringed angularly to squelch the water out, spread out squarely and scrubbed. Repeating this is almost like making music.

Once done, I start to walk towards home, having not brought the car. I am letting the legs walk, walk hard and produce acid. Body has to shut down; my decrepit body is a tough worm, squirms but does not let the gentleman's foot squish it off randomly.

My heels do not deter my pace. I have to ask mother to get rid of that embarrassing memory now where I fell off, all with a pair of 6 inch stilettos. It is too old. I have evolved or my gait has. The Sun scorches down on me but I am all gay about it. I hope to have a headache that will spiral down my spine first, then connect with each of the neurones in my head and explode, my sweet little head bomb. Taut wires will go limp, my body will disassociate from the noises at last, clean silence will rise up like dust. My head will be a messy freak kitchen. My body will crumble, will fall like a thin, weightless paper man. The remote for that bomb is hidden in a golden, gooey haystack. For now, I walk.

I do my usual people watching. I spot a little kid with a running nose, wanting candy and getting rebuffed. His mother with the pointed nose pretends that she has had enough. But an extraordinarily beautiful child like that can demand a van of candies and bloody get it. However, I suppress my maternal instincts and move on. I have too large problems invading my head which are not as easy as candies, kids and their reproving mothers.

Overall, I can safely declare that I am in a mood for violence today.

* * *

As soon as I reach, I drop the bags and run to the wardrobe. I pull out one of your t-shirts and bury my face into it. I inhale and murmur your name.

For someone for who more love was always less, I am sure feeding on a whole lot of crumbs.

The Half-conversation and More Vagueness

The phone in my apartment rings. The alien sound hits me like a sledgehammer. Nobody calls at that number anymore apart from T. But this is not her 'hissy' hour yet. She has gone to destroy someone else's afternoon for all I know. For a moment I debate and then rush to it. I do not understand the desperation.

My tentative hello dissolves in the low rumbling voice that follows. This is not your voice. Not at all.

'Do not ask me who I am' he says.

I chew my lower lip and contemplate.

'Who are you?' I ask

'This is about you' he continues

I am certain this is a crank call and I do not hang up. So it must seem to an onlooker that I am willing to talk about me to a stranger. I toy with the phone cord and say nothing. His breath is raspy. He is the first new person I am interacting (if I can call it an interaction) with.

'I am right here. Take your time'

I can laugh at the absurdity of it all. This feels like a teenage-slasher movie-prelude. I really need more adventures in my life. This is getting ridiculous.

Disconnect.

*   *   *

Nerves are shot. The grand plans to finish my measly work are gone. All I need now is to have myself fired from the contract. Pursuits are wasted if distractions come so easy. This is a fairy tale Sunday which dismisses purpose with a kind whip.

*   *   *

Sunday afternoons are odd. We are already swimming in the fear of Monday. The air is thick with something, it feels like a slab of porridge that can be cut through with a knife. That piece of porridge you will not eat later.

Suddenly I despise life's restrictions. I cannot be invisible, I cannot fly, I cannot torch anything I want to, I cannot shape shift. I do not have hypnotic prowess like you. Are these normal Sunday afternoon thoughts?

As I walk the streets, I fail to metaphorically impersonate someone today. The hollowness, the glutinous centre suddenly starts talking. It says that there is no escape, that I am only buying time. Everyone else is occupied, I cannot replete the deficiency by assuming someone else's completeness. It asks me not to build my life on another myth.

I do not blame people who stare and move away hastily from me. Only the children look fascinated. Madness is still appealing to the innocent.

'Do not grow up' I tell them silently.

*   *   *

I make myself sit on an empty park bench and watch as the world wades through to get there, here, somewhere, nowhere. From what I have seen, destinations change once we arrive. I can tell them so but they will never believe. Well, naivety has its pleasure and price.

There is a tic in my mind which is refusing to go. It is like I know something but I do not know what it is. Very vague remembrance, like a ball of wool, gone too far off, the kitten took it really far this time playing with its paws, and we cannot even see the tiniest knot of wool anywhere. But the mind is a pair of itchy hands, wanting it seen again. So the tic stays alive, ticking, looking like a zit, full of promising revealing revelation, ready to pour out pus at a prick but that will not happen anytime soon.

Someone comes and sits beside me. I am instantly annoyed. Can I not have something totally as mine for a while? I do not look at him and I do not want him to look at me but I can guess he is a man from his trousers. I deliberately look in front.

A one-eyed man is feeding the birds. I envy his mirth. Imagine to have the chaos of the world halved, a room with half a window. My absorption falters and I focus back on the trousers. They have dark blue pinstripes, look well worn but are not frayed at the edges.

I get up on my feet and start walking briskly towards my apartment, leaving the faceless pinstripe trouser man behind.

*   *   *

As I kick off my shoes, I seriously consider getting my head shaved. I do not also miss the fact that I seem to have missed something glaringly vital. The tic ticks.

The Lull

Today is one of those days when nothing happens. Even if something does happen, it is forgettable; it dies before it begins to happen. It dies as a foetus. It dies when it is just a neural discharge, just beginning to sip into a vessel that collects the sap that gets circulated through the vascular network of an idea. I do not even feel like moving. Yet, this is not tranquil stillness. This is an undefined state of disturbance; bizarre suspension with my body parts arranged in erratic positions; my face in between my thighs, my genitalia evenly patched on one of my shoulders, one of the hands standing utterly still, placed precariously on my nose, and the other hand balancing the whole grotesque act. My legs are missing.

The violet of the room seems an ugly gaudy shade right now. The plants seem dry and almost withering. I seem like a mass of impotency. These are not safe feelings, I am unsafe to myself. I live in this shell called a house, which has stopped being a cocoon. It is no longer the home I used to return to. It is an abandoned tenement without a soul.

When my fall breaks, I find myself pieced as before on a moist and slippery bed. I am a lizard slithering over it. My legs, too long and gawky. My body feels heavy, my voice seems hoarse. I make a dash to the mirror and observe my face. It looks porous and unhealthy, my shirt seems ill-fitting and my hair, coarse. This is hardly poetic. You have taken everything with you. I raise my unshaved arms to touch my face. It reminds me of the golden brown hair of yours. You were such a hirsute, maddeningly beautiful man.

I think I am losing my mind for the eleventh time.

*   *   *

I finally see you around the corner. Your face is exactly the way it always is, removed and away. As I come nearer, you pretend not to see me first. I try not to feel the crushing blow to my heart. I look at you imploringly but it does not penetrate anything. Your stoical demeanour cuts through the flesh. I can hear it. Chop chop chop!

But I do not withdraw. I cannot. I realize with a jolt, that you are the only person I love.

I open my mouth to say something but I only mumble. You finally fix your gaze on me.

'Things just happen with me' you say

'Don't say that, please don't say that!'

I understand that I am screaming but I cannot stop it. The scream is a palpable force, like a demon with tentacles, exceeding me. It is pounding and reducing me. And all it wants to say is 'Don't say that!'

'Things just happen with me'

You shrug and say again.

The scream rises a notch, reverberates and bursts into flames.

*   *   *

My heart thuds against my ribs as I wake up in a pool of sweat. When I fall asleep, I have this as my dream. Sanity is measured, insanity is seamless. No one can determine its girth, it expands as one contracts. I was relatively sane; I did not cuss at women and children at the theatre, I did not piss on the roads. I was relatively sane, I put on nice clothes and only made love behind closed doors and screamed moderately.

The shrilling of the phone reminds me what awoke me in the first place. I feel really mad at it and equally grateful. Duality is a strange thing. One hates it in others only to find it in themselves. Or maybe I am splitting into being more than just the one I was. May be there is a dichotomous uprising in me, forcibly shelling me into distinct pieces I may or may not decipher. Like, did Dr. Jekyll really understand Mr. Hyde? Did he understand how he created the abomination and lived a bifurcated life, a strange choice considering how we all innately strive towards virginity of life and people. Always a virgin girl over a promiscuous, well worn woman.

I pad across to the phone with reluctance. I feel a terrible fierceness breeding within, like a maniac set loose after years of confinement. The instant I take the call, I know it is him. The same heavy breathing seems to permeate through the room.

'Unravelling is never easy' he says.

I purse my lips as I feel the vein in my forehead distend. I wish to sever his windpipe.

'Listen to me freak and listen to me well' I begin. 'I do not have time for the likes of you. If you don' t have anything else to do, go die'

I stop to catch my breath. One has to admit that what I said was pretty tacky.

'Dying is equally uneasy' he says softly.

I gather the phone with the wires in my hand and hurl it across the room.

*   *   *

The next few hours I spend trying to fix my almost dead phone. I mourn my impulse and try being the best mechanic I can be.

We should never break things we have to mend ourselves.

Hardly a Wake-up Call

I am a logophile. Love for words, is a natural instinct. Dissecting them comes effortlessly, like chefs knead pounds of soft dough. However, the path of professionally loving words is a difficult one. Despite which, a few years ago, quite miraculously I published a short anthology of poems, morbidly harrowing poems, to moderate success. The editor was a friend of a friend, with both connections and money and an incredible love for T. I say I earned it, that my fingers went quite dark writing, erasing, re-writing those lines seven hundred times. But who knows? Every real writer must have swollen fingers, I agree. Mine are no different. My fingers are bent, lined and fatigued just like those hundred unknown unpublished poets in back alleys.

My poems, even though trivial, had the dignity of the first frustrations of a naïve, hopeful writer. Faint creative jubilations, not overpowering, just the lightest treads, carefully sanctioned. Owing to this delicate balance perhaps, it was not a failure like it was quantitatively expected. So that was that, I wrote a book which got published and I could call myself a writer. With it came the demand that I write another, less personal, more finesse and I said 'yes, yes, yes'.

However, words congeal. And they did in my head, the writer's greatest enemy. It trickled down in spurts and understandably 'the epic book/ the brilliant second' did not become an immediate delivery. In this case, I wrote a few lines, felt unhappy, re-wrote them seven hundred times and deleted again. Shifting perspectives became a bane, sane enlightenment became spurious. Words did not gurgle in my pen anymore; pens were stray friends, riddled in small talks and not the story of their lives. Till I can drain the ink the way I should, I pay my bills with odd freelance work that lets me soak in the morning summer Indian heat, play with my time in unforgivable ways. At the back of my head the noose of the book hangs still, always in the light of my mind.

Meanwhile, I keep receiving occasional calls reminding me that I have not been dutiful and that the preliminary advance given to me was a gesture that was not reciprocated in kind. I usually listen while words spit and ravage in my head. Today's call is no different. During the initial split second quietness that predominates the beginning of a conversation, I sense her sharpness as always.

'I will not mince words.' she says

She never does.

'You cannot be on unlimited sabbatical'

Her voice though not heavy is certainly not soft. It has qualities that can range from sweet to extreme citric. With me, it is on troubled pastures, extremely detached without the hastiness. She masticates each word and extracts my fear like a syringe. I know I have been spared so far only because she has chosen not to sabotage her feelings for T.

'I know you are recovering but you are already liable for the breach of your contract which stipulated that you submit at least half of the new work two months ago. However owing to the respect I have for our . . . common friend, I am willing to give you an unheard of extension of a month to produce the same'

I do not understand what she means by I am recovering; does she think I suffer from some enigmatic illness?

"Use your time well"

A click and end of conversation.

The last pawn of meagre kindness. I inhale sharply.

People do not talk to me. They do not wait to hear what I am meant to say. What they are supposed to hear from me. What they need to hear from me. I am a voiceless device, I move my mouth, very hard, the contours of my mouth stretching from side to side, silently lip syncing to what I must have said.

It will be good to remember that a song-less device is an unforgiving cyborg.

*   *   *

In these days, kindness shocks me, almost appals. It is a misfit.

When good things in life stop appealing, should I start getting worried? I cannot ask them to stop and wait for you, so that we can share them together. This, that, and that moments are gone. You were never there to feel them on your fingertips and they never paused. I could not save them for you. Not that you asked me to. It is a habit of yesterday.

The evening is pretty where stars look like crystals. All people I see appear unusually happy. They are voluble and animated. I wish I had someone to turn my head towards and talk. Just talk. About mundane, oddities, trifles, odds and ends, bliss, hope, all good things.

Amidst the gale and laughter, the bitter effervescence of unknown joy, the twinkle of a rundown CD shop catches my eye. Without even having to scan, I know what I want.

It is good knowing what you want. Knowledge fosters irrepressible sunshine in the white vacancy of your heart. There is something really ominous about that sterile whiteness. It is in actuality, the very core of pretend darkness.

*   *   *

I rub the newness of the disc against my cheek. As the song begins lushly, there is an old knot of butterflies in my stomach. Can I not have one cause to live for everyday?

I cannot die now. The knot has to live, for old time's sake.

Same Old

This is THE pattern: climax to be followed by a very powerful anti-climax. The severity of the anti-climax squeakily cleans the happy crumbs of the divine climax. My climax in this particular incident was a slow train of rising vascular and aural spasms, absolutely asexual but a tyrannical climax nevertheless. A long awaited one, undiluted, away from the reaches of the quintessential pleasures of sex, drugs and rock and roll. It was a music CD. *Travis' s 'A Man Who'*.

For the past half an hour, I have been looking at the plastic wrapper of the CD which I bought yesterday. The wrapper is a fisted, transparent ball of dismissal, occupying a small corner of my bed, shrinking in humiliation. I pick it up, iron it out with my hands and place it on the table. I loll my head backwards and hear T mutter as she struggles with some sauce.

Yes, catastrophe has struck, in black fishnet stalking, her banter in black smoke, her hair in black freeness, un-silent. Too many cigarettes, in her mouth, in ashtrays, windowsills, basin, transgressing fumes into my opaque mind.

She invades me like her wardrobe, coming in and going out unannounced, sifting through my head like a librarian, selecting facets and details, asking questions, discarding, accepting, crippling me with veracity, honouring me with nothing.

She says,

'I brought you my smoke palace'

Her chatter is more philosophical than one would expect. Previously, it was forked; now it's strictly linear. It speaks of my devastation, interlaced with her own. However, her cynicism is so dark that it is hard to fathom the inherent pain in it. People perceive her more as a dark mistress than an unfortunate maiden. But since, we are bound by invisible necromantic coils since a very long time, since I am on the inside of the concrete kingdom, she is my bastard twin. Often we just stare at each other, without lips moving or limbs, having telepathic conversations about how we ended our worlds, how we burned the grass, smelled the yellow turf, and still ran on the fields thinking it would go green again if we kept running, through the wind and the fumes. It did not and here we are, in our dark city, grappling with calamities, with our quirks and deficiencies. In this city, within the real city we live in, we claw at each other because that is the protocol. In here we have never experienced dictionary love; in here, definitions are catapulted far away as nothing about this dark city is familiar.

'Do you want to talk about how you crashed down? the smoke was almost a halo around her mouth

'Again?'

'Again. Did you think you would be happy with a man only motivated by glory?'

'I did not think it was only about that. He was hypnotic, he was a sorcerer, he made me a believer. That was enough.'

T dismisses the sauce bowl and dives into the sofa next to me. Cigarettes immediately lit, the round face of tobacco glowing unevenly as her lungs inhale the sooty rush. She looks like a smoky serpent nestled in my house. Uncrossing her legs, she spreads them further where they almost usurp my sofa space and wriggle her wicked toe nails.

'You know' she begins huskily *'I thought you always knew our perfect world is the alternate world with the red Sun. Remember the picture I painted when we were still kids, that was for us and our*

second life. This life is the imposter. We are just supposed to live it out, meet death, and cross over. Look at all the destruction here, look at my infertility, are we supposed to live here where I cannot have a protruding womb?'

'I did not have to live your version of our lives, T'. I interject 'There was real milk in my milky way, you will not believe'.

Then comes the theatrics; she fills the room with her hoarse laughter, black crude oil pouring out from her mouth onto my floor.

*   *   *

T's father abandoned both her mother and her when she was six. They started living with her maternal grandparents whose furore lacked the decency which would have eventually doused it. For their three meals and a room, life became an odd game. All relatives gathered to objectify her sin, and her sinful produce: the girl child. *Pishis,* Para'r Didas, random *Kakimas*, each haunted by their joblessness and kitchens, circular prattles, intoxicated by afternoon slumber, cradled by vicious idle curiosity, hovered over for their real-time matinee. The main topics revolved around *'did the husband leave her for another woman? Probably a more literate one?'* , *'did she lie and leave her husband instead?'* , *'is this child even theirs?'* , *'my good karma has saved me from having some disgraceful children, I did some good rearing'*.

T's grandparents stood by and listened to the vile, and did not say a word. Their snarky expression clearly advocated their own purity against their daughter's filth.

This is when T's mother wept in her room, while biting into the seams of her sari's *aanchol* and we used to run off to behind our favourite bush, and forced our crayons to produce red, blue, yellow till they bent and broke. It was during those days that T drew me the Red Sun. Despite what she called it, it was a ghastly orange orb with uneven peripheries; metaphorically it was the land of the angry fair Sun which protected angry people who migrated to their planet. That, was our childhood fantasia.

T was never a sublime child; when she was angry, her canines showed and she shook her brilliant mop of darkest hair. She was a devastation waiting to grow and erupt into moist golden lava. Her volatile life was a change for me, it was an attraction. My house was full of simpletons who inhabited in mediocrity and restrictions, a quiet rundown life that put fear first and aspirations later. We ate fish in the afternoons, the inexpensive kind with a lot of fish bones, some vegetable mash with huge bowls of *daal*. Meat was rarely brought and the days when it came, it was a massive treat. We would gnaw on the bones, suck out the last vestiges of marrow and still not let go.

My mother was a plain woman, with neatly parted hair, visible *sindoor* and usually a chequered *sari* that did not inspire. My father was a docile man with occasional flaring temper, a husband who did not seem to have either lust or love for his wife. He talked to her about the rising expenses, the Congress, his views on how Congress could spawn more, as they rightfully should in West Bengal, how he could not manage clothes for all the relatives with his *Pujo* budget and equally un-amorous chitchats. My mother quietly listened to all he had to say, with glazed eyes, braiding my hair. Her bangles rattled against each other and her thin lips formed a dry line on her face as she concentrated on my hair, each strand, each follicle. Her lack of literacy gave her the right to silence to everything that happened in our household; to my father unapologetically breaking wind in the morning, to the stinking beans he insisted she cooked every day, to my friendship with the wild child, to the world drowning in a plume of soft, muddy hysteria. Only recently she shows a kind of slow anger, sultry, adhesive but checked and only retained for me. It must have been burning under the embers for years.

When I met T, I was teleported to a different world, a chaotic carousel where strange things happened. She still does that to me.

Later, when she was 16, her mother started living with a tormented but a brilliant Bengali poet, while none of his poems ever reflected her. She was called a 'fangirl' or a 'Groupie' but she claimed he had married her. She ran around with his periodicals, and poem cut outs from magazines, and yelled them out from street corners as a form of marketing. By then, none of us really considered her a human being wholly anymore.

'You were saved. You are better off without men who want to write cyberpunk fiction. May be you were a blow up doll for him, one he would have wanted to inflate at will and deflate mostly'

'I wanted to write that novel with him you know'

'But you didn' t'

*　　*　　*

The most frightening feeling is to feel that I will forget how you looked. How your side of the bed smelt. How you plodded across the room and said 'Mamma' when you saw me. How your 2-day-old stubble felt. How I felt when you explained to me how you felt about me.

Somewhere, I can hear Deftones go:

' Cause tonight I feel like more,

Tonight I feel like more'

Yes, it did not kill me when you left. Yes, it totally killed me when you left.

Trauma Inc.

One day we wake up to find the Sun cut out or painted black. Overnight someone did it, peeling the planet off its solar sucrose–a vicious man, no doubt, deriding life's irregular heat. As plants shrivel, we think of how we led our lives, how we drank cheap *Mod*, how we swam at the deep end of the lake and looked at fish run.

(A) The old man always hated his wrinkled face. It crinkled up too much when he smiled. However, the familiar sight of him walking down the steps to the *ghat* in the early morning for his daily cold dip, draped in his favourite loincloth is oddly reassuring.

(B) The metro station is hyperventilating with millions of feet blurring its soul. Feet, feet, feet (long, unshaven, stocky), arms (sinewy, thin, old), hair (wispy, thick, uncombed), faces (poke marked, soft, grimy), flipping coins, rushing past bodies, no one looks at no one. Everyone on a fast track, reaching dark places with light.

(C) The young kid loves his water toy gun. People squeal and he squeezes his trigger harder. Nothing else in his experience makes adults laugh like that, like him. Tumble over on the grass, squint their eyes; their laughter rises in the heat, like water bubbles, transparent and full of the world.

(D) The girl is alone. Whether she is lonely or not is debatable. Her disability is obscured by her will to live. Sometimes, things are too murky for her but she lives through them. She always knows, at the end of it, she has to see another day. She is getting closer to the pulsating centre of where it all began and will possibly end.

One day we wake up to find the Sun pieced back in its place. It glistens and you cannot stare at it, not that you ever could easily. The plants begin their photosynthesis, it has been a while. In the temporary days of darkness, solids were still eaten and gold was still gold. Very less changed, except that people now knows that even the Sun is changing.

*   *   *

If at all, life is ALL about not making sense. Like this gummy dream which sticks to the inside of my cranium, utterly regardless of whether I want it as a memory. Sometimes I wonder if we even realize the complex machines that we are. It is an inter-web of neurons, pulses, blood cells, fat, tissues, tendons, cartilages, muscles, bones-this incredible maze we carry with us around all the time, without deciphering, without cognition, without recognizing the greatest fear-that any of this can explode and our little spinning meandering universes with its people, trees, dogs will all come to a fatal standstill. Our carefully spoken words, our insignificant marriages, the drives late into the abysmal nights, the sudden spurts of lust, will all collapse into a single moment of non existence.

I look at T, delicately snaked on my sofa, mouth half open, eyes moving ever so slightly, carving monsters in her head, gutting them open and flinging their intestines everywhere. Her face, even in sleep, is slightly angry, honouring her intense demeanour, an undying warrior, a dying woman. My friend.

*   *   *

One of the strangest feelings I had with you was this moment when I was watching you sleep. I was thinking how would it be if I died knowing that you loved me when you did not. If that would be an honest death. If there would be any honour in that release. If me dying, unknown to the truth, would make my passing lesser than the man/woman before me. Would I linger in the afterlife, unable to pass on completely, haunted literally? In our urban myths, the ones my mother told me mostly to coerce me into finish eating would be of many such women, or *Aatmas*, long haired, frantic with something unforgotten. May be a simple question. Usually simple things are not as lucid, there is a deeper battle waiting to be fought. All the histories we never came to know, the questions that ambled in and out of our lives, some quick, some terribly stretched.

There used to be a red bricked poor man's cottage styled tenement next to our house. It had been abandoned and the rumour was that a child killed himself there by accidentally drinking poison. While the tragedy was inconsolable, what always flustered me was the state of the house. Due to rather close proximity, I could see everything inside. Nothing was removed; everything used to lay there untouched, like in the middle of a regular day. Door ajar, pot on the floor, overturned, *Moshari* half hung on the bed, bed soiled and unmade after a night's sleep, windows unsealed. My mother said that was the last day they were ever seen, any of them. After the child collapsed, the mother frantically gathered him in her arms and ran and no one (not even the father) ever came back. The house was deserted in an instant, their story beside our house stopped rolling forever. There was never a playback. Can people really uproot their lives of years and exit without a notice? As far as I was concerned, the parents became as much as apparitions as the child. I hated the house's un-obscurity, its lack of privacy, an inimical past floating next to our conventional present.

That night while you slept unaware, I thought of the house, their tenants of so many years ago, you and deaths. I felt brave and opted for the real over the illusion.

Courage is another foolish sentiment. You never know what you are bracing yourself for, till it is knocking the wind out of you.

*   *   *

There is nothing to repair. It was a simple dream. All I wanted was 30 odd years with you.

Was I too young?

The Endless Odyssey

Today, I wake up happy. I couldn't believe it for a while till I had to. Life is so simple when I am happy; my alter-ego rests, I feel feminine, oracle T does not scare me with her prophesies, I can sing, I feel there is a future for me, clean like a fresh soft egg, one that wriggles if you nudge its body lightly. I can feel my pores opening up, letting in a different spirit, mangle-free, past-less, untangled like straight silken hair.

In the past seven weeks, I have obsessively bought several stacks of pencils. I have no use of them, may be T can use some (she is an occasional painter when she is not mad or inebriated) but generally, they were bought purposelessly. They lie on my desk, sullen. I wonder if they walk out of the boxes when I am sleeping at night. Roam around the room, taking careful dainty steps, itching for paper and their right to be sharpened. Their right to words, images, scribbles, doodles. Their right to determine their vocation, their place in the world. Their right to know the world like they should, however they like. All in all, I think they like their lives, when there is always a rewind. Write something, keep it, scratch it, rub it off, tear off the page, incinerate it, pass it through a shredder, and everything is gone. Start again. Like new. Pencils therefore have no guilt. They are not born conscientious because they do not require to be.

Loathe a person, as much as you need to, let the acid flow freely from your hand to the paper. Write intensely, with conviction, see red, tell everybody just how the brass hit her mouth and how her blood and drool took a plunge for the carpet. Tell us how you felt the rush fill your heart, and how the sweep of adrenaline at the sight of violence made your day. Tell us all. The pencils will not be held responsible.

*   *   *

The fan is not behaving itself today. It is making the most vicious noise and barely spinning. In the Bengali bourgeoisie household there are always fans, in multiples too. Additionally, air conditioners make my skin scratchy and horribly dry. Hence, the fan must work. I look at it while it groans. A typical ceiling fan these days is modern looking, with sharp, slim blades. However, a typical ceiling fan in the days of my forefathers was remarkably different. It used to be a flamboyant affair, with ostentatious blades and often a sweeping decorative fixture over the top of the motor. Those were the days when people celebrated siesta, cracked their knuckles forever and believed that good karma fetched good. These are the new days now.

These ceiling fans always remind me of my mother. Back in those days, during power outages I would grow restless and she would start fanning me with a paper hand fan; her slim wrist, veined yet strong, kept flipping it from side to side, till my body grew cool and I fell asleep. Her right arm, moving through the day ceaselessly, still became a powerhouse for her child.

My mother now, is quite a different woman. The thin dry line of her mouth has become softer, and her body surer, fuller, with vitality that only the right kind of aloneness can bring. Even though she mourned deeply for my father when he passed away, along with it came a long winding tenuous journey of the hole. Alice was not the only one. Her body was scratched and torn when she arrived at the end finally. She became an estranged matriarch, a complicated, forlorn evolution of a journey of her own choice.

The day we decided to live separately, I was twenty five with young blood coursing through. She was fifty one with new blood coursing through.

Unknown almost, probably slightly darker than mine. She let me go with the swiftness of a felon's death from the Hangman's noose. How long must it have taken? 3-5 minutes?

To this T had to say, *'You are not the young bird here. Look at her plump feathers, she is ready to fly now. Without you.'*

I was the abandoned dish bowl with faeces.

*   *   *

The pencils look all regular, even, unstoppably barricaded. Un-chiselled or chiselled, they can be used to gouge eyes out, with proper deftness. They are art's foot soldiers. They are clandestine pawns ready to rip your heart apart.

I like pencils because you liked them. There were many things I liked just because they were your favourites. But it was not out of any lover's obligation. It was as uncomplicated as not being able to dislike anything that you liked.

When I buy these pencils, it does not have any pattern. I disconnectedly do things as and when I remember them. I do them not because I have to. There is no real purpose to anything. These disjointed activities will perhaps take me somewhere. Open an unseen door. Because more often than not, I do not know what I am supposed to do anymore. I have no idea.

Hey! There is no method to this madness. Do you hear?

*   *   *

We are rolling down the stairs. We are laughing, it does not hurt. Your curls and mine are a mesh together. I feel them with my hands and entangle them even further. I never want them to extricate. I want your hair blue and mine red.

'Dear darling scientist, this is such savage alchemy'

We keep bouncing down the stairs. We are curled up in an exquisite foetal position, the way only we can. My mouth is near your Adam's apple and as I see you swallow, I lean forward and kiss it. You gulp harder now and pull my hair. Tufts of my hair in your palm and you bring them close and sniff.

'Sweet home Alabama'

Your voice trembles and cracks but you don't stop saying it and I don't stop you.

'Sweet home Alabama'

'Sweet home Alabama'

'Sweet home Alabama'

As you keep chanting, our hair slowly turns to water, it fills my nostrils and you quietly drown.

*　　*　　*

I cannot stop shivering. My body is on fire. I am aroused. I close my eyes and try to dream that again. All I have are snippets of a garbled dream but one which took me closest to you in months. I touch my hair and it is only mine. This dream was my temporary surrogate child; intangible, fake. You are filling me with an unholy smoke that is dissolving my skin. There is nothing to thaw, I am smoke now.

*　　*　　*

The greatest thing about you is that you made me hungry.

The greatest thing about you is that you made sure you remain the only hunger.

Yet Another Monologue

There has to be a ban on liking/loving people easily. It makes little sense. For the longest time I have been that. At once touched if a lady smiled or a dog wagged its tail too hard. I will like to think that is how I was. I am trying to think I am different now. Enclosed in a room, I am trying to prove that I am fearless, emotionless. T is hovering near me and chanting Nietsze: *'When you look into an abyss, the abyss also looks into you'* . After an hour of hearing that, I am feeling like I am transforming into the abyss. I feel like a hollow and vast space, incomprehensibly abound. People, birds, boulders, debris, sparkling sand are all passing through me, unaware of the unrestricting abyss, disturbingly inhuman, honestly unafraid. T is right. This is what was to become; I looked into an abyss and I have ecome one. The world stays or not, I remain the ilent, murderous abyss that stops no fall.

* * *

While undergoing several perversities, people inherit mutations. Once in a dream I turned into a gargoyle and also had blue fins. In real life, mutations are more severe. Real life fantasies are all grotesque. Around two years ago, a married friend of T lost his wife in a hit and run just six months into their marriage. It was an instantaneous death that must have been relieving for the dead wife but the husband was plundered beyond human consolation. So, he mutated. He paid a whore each night, to dress like his wife and lay still on the spot on the road where she died. This went on for a while till the police got a sniff of it and arrested him. After he was released on bail, he carried out the same in his house. All he would do while the "double" lay still, was to tell her *'You should not have done this'*. He repeated this ritual every night for an hour till he felt cleansed, sane and willing to wake up the next day. After a year, he just disappeared pretending to go on a road trip.

Mutation can be difficult because most people do not realize that they have mutated while everyone around them can. Basic mutations are hard to notice, occur in spurts and are only visible to the most stringently observing. Extraordinary mutations are usually too spectacular to be muted. I have been

always been intrigued by mutated people; I recognize
more sense in their mania than the regular social
violence, bigotry and misogyny. When people discover
this sympathy of mine, they are usually repulsed.
What they mean is, they cannot see the light beyond
the swarthiness. That is acceptable. For me, I will
always understand a serial killer's motivation
(considering his history of inconceivable childhood
abuse, fear and pain) to a random power-play rape
of a woman by a normal man (or men) with normal
upbringing, probably with a normal family with a
normal wife and two normal kids. The former is a
case of mutation and the latter is a case of
senseless blood/sex lust. However that is not to say
there are no fake mutants.

You say clothes make a woman and I say not,
never, ever to have your grimy hand shove a rod
up her vagina while you feel victory in your
filthy masquerade. YOUR frustration against your
OWN incapacity does not sanction you the right to
violate a woman's pristine body, her choice of
wilful sex, her right to ANY clothes, her right
to movement with ANY man. People scream chemical
castration and I say lets bust this long standing
system of perverse pain infliction and start with
ending the debate. There is no education for the
soulless. Kill the fuzzy logic.

*   *   *

Often I remember the people I have hurt. Their
grief seemed insignificant then. I seemed right. My

impulses seemed more correct. What I was, if plainly put, was selfish. Pain was always less when it was someone else's. Somehow, now I have difficulty in accepting my past self worshipping. For a while, I had done so much of what I was not. If I consider the karmic cycle, the dots do connect. Though, I can always run for cover and say 'Fate made me do it'.

This especially reminds me of a friend. Who loved me and I did not love as much. Only to know later that I did but the later was rather late. He had by then, misconstrued and I was beyond recognition for him. There were other external factors furthering his mistaking as well, but that is of no consequence. Had there been no schemers, there would have been no slander. Without any kink, their reason to live would have dissolved. People would have died of straightforwardness. The twist in the tale is the fodder, one cannot refuse them that. Can they? Anyway, this is another story and of too long ago.

Generally, love is senselessly fluid. It drapes the body with a watery sheet, it bloats us. It is like having a watery breakdown, all with your lymph and lymphatic vessels disgorging unrestrained unordered happiness. So while you feel like a happy Phosphorous child, you are actually dismantling yourself into water that is spreading everywhere. Into ducts, out on the streets, into people's homes, under shoes like puddles, over heads like a drizzle, wetting body parts of unknown men, women, children; you are everywhere. You are omnipresent in this love that has taken you apart beautifully and you spread out your eager limbs, like limber tentacles. Now, when it ends, you will have to suck back every part of you that you freely gave away, coagulate, and even after a process of intense solidifying, you will be only a part of what you used to be. You will be a wise carcass, walking barefoot, with a head full of memories, swarming like bees.

*   *   *

What bothers me is, just when it seems like I have arrived somewhere, I have not. Every time, I am hoping that I can exercise my audacity, just the way I always have. Intrinsically, I do not want to change my mould at all. Every time there is a shift, I recoil. Of all I know, I cannot control myself. I am beyond my own scope.

In the morning, I saw people having coffee in a coffee shop. They were too well-dressed to be visiting a coffee shop. I was in my dirty blue pyjamas, which also might have been the reason for the overestimation. As I sipped my coffee, I started to find their assuredness repelling. They seemed to have every hair in place. I wondered if they ever cowered in their rooms and wept. If they ever howled to themselves all night long. If they ever cut themselves on the thighs so that no one else could see. I came back rebuking the sane world.

Back in my hole called home, now I think of the frothy coffee I had. I wonder who made it. And if he/she has a harrowing mother who forces them to have that extra helping of vegetables every night. Or if they brush their hair before they sleep, rinse their mouth, curl their hair before they go on a date, pass by halogen lamps flocked by insects, get on rickety *rickshaws* and give directions to remote places along narrow, bricked lanes, buy scented slim flower garlands for evening home *Pujos*.

I wonder if something as simple as these have been destined too. Like today will be the day, I will go out to have coffee and not make it for myself like all other days. Have I ever taken a single conscious decision then? If I have not, and if this indeed is the rule of the thumb, then I should have no guilt on me. I am as clean as a new born.

I will not be able to hold you responsible for anything. Others will not hold me responsible for anything. Any consequence will never be the result of MY action. Because there is no MY action. Lawyers will go out of business. There are no sinners because there is no sin. We will be doing only what we are to do. Someone has to mow the grass and someone has to rape a 10 year old. Blame the higher puppeteer. Cannot blame the puppets.

I have to be the saddest self-proclaimed philosopher and this is one sickening theory.

Thankfully, there will be no book on this.

A Little Less of You, A Little More of You

Today morning is different. It is the first since that day, where I wake up to feeling nothing. If you ask me, I really cannot say if vacuity feels better. In a way, movement is reassuring, no matter how aimless. Friction reasserts life. Lying here on the bed, I feel displaced from myself. I have a body and yet I am truncated. It is different from the time when I felt all my body parts were randomly organized like a Frankenstein.

If grief is a motion, I want to write a poem on it. To have people turn and say, 'Sorrow made her a poet'. To have something more than my mother mourning over my dead body, a fiery cremation of no fire.

This reminds me of a blog post I wrote a couple of weeks back. The blog post was a result of limited control. I was unhappily fondling misery. But post examination of it, I found it unhealthily superficial. It looked so flamboyant. What is it with us people that we cannot put our pain simply? Why could I not write 'I feel heart-broken without you'? Instead I picked and chose words even as I wept. Intrinsically, we cannot do without grandiosity. We want our pain to be magnificent and be applauded for it too. I am ashamed.

I am ashamed that I did not stop to look for recognition in a piece of prose which was supposed to chronicle something intimate. The personal was made to be a public outcry. Will I ever be a woman who can knit and watch a cat play with a ball of wool?

*   *   *

Gossamers are delicately spun oldness. They hang loose in the corners of rooms, secretly famished for the past, clearly biding their time, before they are 'cleared' for new space for their descendants. They always find their spots, and are relentlessly alive even when people curse their dysfunction. More than strings of dirt, they exemplify past life, memories of interlocking flesh. They also glorify loneliness.

Like most other people, I have my understanding of loneliness. I have been brave about it, and very afraid. Loneliness I imagined is a lonely man. Wears a tall hat, (the kind I watched Anglo Indian grandfathers wear in the evening, made of tweed I believe, when I was a little frock wearing kid) and is always polite to the ladies when he meets them. He has a harrowing looking forehead, as that is where he stores the loneliness of the world. He dispatches it globally, but unequally, so one man has only seconds of it, while many others a lifetime. He believes inequality is where he sprung from, so disparate distribution is only a part of it. He is a harmless man with a mass detonating power of seclusion, silent and truly believable.

When you were with me, loneliness was a fickle friend. Paid visits in parties if you were out of sight for longer than ten minutes. I forgot the drink and paid half attention to conversations. You always reappeared and I never told you of my stupid fears. I could never define that fear.

When you laughed with someone, I wished it was me. I was un-giving when it was you. I had only known to love that ill-fitting way. You always laughed and called me a child. Your child.

I am not against loneliness, rather used to it now. Without it, things look too simple. But there is a difference between 16 year old loneliness and 26 year old loneliness. The latter is more leathery and thick with fear, like old people. It does not mature but decays with time. A shawl, tightly wound, growing warm, warmer, too warm.

I have not grown but the shawl has. If it turns out to be a noose, I will have to try and make a fancy tie out of it.

*   *   *

I can vaguely understand the theory of narcissism. It is beautifully safe. Sincere investments on somebody else do not guarantee sincerity. Somebody else still stays as an independent autonomous unit. You cannot hold them by the collar and demand them to perform. There is also no remote control. One can only hope that it chooses to walk with you. T understands this very well. She always walks alone. She is that mystical Rubik's cube that I have partially deciphered, partially unhooked, partially forgotten, partially healed, partially sculpted, totally will never penetrate, break down into atoms. Even if I do, there will always be her endless hair obscuring my tempered comprehension. Even when I am alone, wisps of her hair float by my chair or clumps clot my drain. Away from their mistress, they ploy to invisibly darken my remaining light. Our love for each other is a bizarre massacre; not totally bizarre or truly a massacre. It is a timeless full moon, a crescent of which is stitched inside of us. It is not wholly circular when we are together, but they are each other's other halves. Hence, we survive year after year, coiled in our own inextricable birth, always sure but never quite settled. With radically different cores, we never merge; we are two scraggy balls of yarn rolling together, indefinitely, on paths we no longer much care about, but are getting bigger with something we are accumulating in these endless rotations nevertheless. I look at her and she looks at me and we are both about to violently eject something out of our wombs, screaming and veined. But for now, we are draped in a false sense of reality, a gelatinous suit that lets us perform our regular duties in faux sanity.

A while back when I spoke to my mother, I let my mind wander. She spoke in undertones. I could detect the cleverly cloaked soreness. I filled our brief conversation with heartless hollow laughter and failed anecdotes.

All I want to do is to empty my body and let my skeletal representation speak on my behalf. Bereft of bodily meat, it will be a simple skeleton, ribbed and hollow, living still, air caressed, vestiges of a bony faraway leftover tomb. White, of course.

*   *   *

This is not entirely system cleansing. This can be called scrubbing but it is not even that. This is not conscious cleaning. This is a random experiment which aims at nothing. It is nothing.

Fail

Once when I was younger, I had a fleeting relationship with an older man. We both wanted wrong things out of each other. I presume, he wanted sex while I was looking for affection, the fatherly kind. When I could not conform to his needs, I fled. I still remember his face while he cried. A grown-up crying inconsolably was scary and I was too young to understand that adults often feel like babies. I was bemused and only slightly saddened. One can say I almost felt next to nothing. Later, Thievery Corporation used to remind me of him. And that was all.

He kept asking me what made me stop loving him and I could not say that I never did. I also did not tell him, that his attempts to get intimate made me

want to break his face. I do not know what made me
seem real to him. As an act of parting fondness, I
allowed myself to kiss his forehead and cringed when
he tried to grope. In an urgent attempt to keep me,
he misconstrued my platonic sensibility and hissed
'Eat me' . Even in misery, he lacked elegance.

Had you said that, I would have ravaged you.
Had you not said anything I would have ravaged you.
There is nothing called inelegance in passion.

*   *   *

T is walking with me. Her long hair is tucked neatly behind her elf like ears, her feet striding ahead of me. I watch her neck, a little short to be swan like, but beautifully tilted, green veins palpitating against the paleness, lacking in monstrosity of any kind. I start drawing the anatomy of her larynx, thinking it might be a gaudy shade of pink, getting punctured every time she swallows, or prickly like an inimical porcupine tree.

Our walks are legendary; when we start twirling too much in vacuum, unable to stop the hexed spin, our hands missing each other, our hands failing to grapple with our own uncontrolled revolution, we let go of our bodies, and let them levitate. Levitation swells our bodies, and the expanding heaviness plants our bodies finally on the ground. Then we calmly dress ourselves and let ourselves out for a walk.

We walk on this anonymous pebbled street we know which bends, and turns, and twists and takes us into a remote clearing where all one can see is a tiny, forsaken, derelict brown coloured shop, made of straw, an amputated torso of a body unknown. This shop that sells *lebu chaa,* some cheap varieties of flower and petal shaped biscuits in glass boxes with tin covers is our secret haven. A sole candle flickers always behind the glass boxes and a silent, wrinkled woman noiselessly moves. This is where we stop to breathe, and T looks back at me and motions me to sit next to her on one of the wood stumps. The Sun is clear on the sky, gentle but not without indignity. It is making her hair sparkle. It is usually like this whenever we come here for our guilt free conversations.

Here we are inept, here we are people with our open boxes of delusion. Here we scatter everything with our hands like confetti, wilfully, and let the air play with it. We like the savage dance.

'We are here again'

'We are always here'

For the next twenty minutes, we don't talk. But it is good silence. Silence embodying a peculiar softness of not having to talk.

We are two strangers in a strange meeting; this is how we start. You start twirling in front of us, both T and I watch. The leaves protect your body like a cocoon and you start talking. *You tell us of your ambitions, your pain, your deceptions, your intricate plans for yourself and the unexpected ingénue—too artless for your taste, too mediocre for your mountain, too soft for your bed. You gave her sudden profane reality, an unusual gift as a lover and she died. But you rose as a king, conquered a few lands, rode on horses and made graceless love to a lot of promiscuous women. You do not regret anything. Simple human sacrifices are obligatory in the path of greatness. You say it is okay to start small fires and not douse it afterwards; if it wrecks a forest, you cannot be held responsible for it. It was small and useful and you had no idea it would grow that big.*

T smiles at me as my head grows moist at your monologue. Slowly, your body un-ensconces from the foliage and spins till it disappears. T gets us two plastic cups of tea and lets me stay alone for three minutes. She always says that it is not too long and not too less.

'You heard him' she says

'I know him, I know that.'

'Will it be closure this time? Her voice is surreal. Her question already has a ring of the answer to it.

I feel like the mountain you were talking about is in my throat and I cannot swallow. I think my larynx is going to burst into a dirty mist, so dirty that T would have trouble finding way back home. So violent an explosion that this place would stop existing, the silent woman would screech for the first time, and you would have created fire again.

*   *   *

Since I have been back, I have locked myself in the toilet, even though the rooms are empty. The toilet is for a more private kind of privacy. I sit on the toilet seat, suspend my legs for a while and then wrap them around themselves. The commode is particularly white tonight, against the darkness of my skin. What am I? This mass of dark, unfulfilled molecules, mushrooming towards becoming an animal, a collapsible mute animal, with no further story to tell, not of her own anyway.

I pay close attention to the water dripping from the tap. It does not care for my stare, presence, life, death, anything. If I die here right now and if two days later the police breaks the door down and hauls my body out, water will still drip from the tap, like it is now. No inconsistency like humans. It has to drip, it is the only thing it has to do. It is fraught with nothing but this peculiar sense of responsibility.

Unexpectedly I feel the pain of the world. Especially of those I have not met and will never meet. Perhaps a lonely kid, whose nose ran and did not have anyone to hold her. I can see her, with her little torn mind, kicking at pebbles. Her angry little foot swollen and tired.

I rock back and forth, wanting to tell her that she is not unseen, that I can see her. But she keeps slipping into a crazy dance of blackness. I cannot stop.

I fail her. Failing is not new.

Run, Find, Run

Life—there is the haystack and there is no needle. So, basically we will find nothing. But the haystack is a constant lure to want to find the needle. The needle is no ordinary needle. Its existence is elusive but the elusion is emphatic. It makes you want to find it, but in all possibility, it will never be there to be found. One will run to find it but cannot run away from finding it. Bad needle?

Is it all about acceptance, then? That I do not accept the things I do not want and cannot have the things I do want? Does it make me ungrateful and unkind to the things that are there and willing to be mine? But will that be love? It seems like being an opportunist but people seem to call that practicality. Something must be wrong with me and the world. Or may be none of us. Just a case of all of us hating each other and wanting to establish our uniqueness.

When I do not think about you, I think about these. Like riddles, I try to solve them. When I think I have found a suitable answer, I feel pleased. But I am a philosopher without a philosophy. I belie my ideas and say I have moved on with the world. Consistency is foolishness, I have been told. And taught. Consistency is a remarkable dreamy hypothesis. If ever found, it should be kept in a museum—admired, let to collect precious dust.

I dip my toe in the bath tub. The water is cold. I like warm water, very warm water. But today, I do nothing about the cold. I do not wince as the water laps against my shoulders. It stings me like a hornet. I dunk my head under and exhale slowly. I see my watery image—body, white and pale, my shoulder blades look exceptionally bony, I do not turn into a fish. The watery film makes everything seem unreal. I just become two pair of eyes watching my torso float. It is fascinating if one can stand the apparent disunion. Breathless, I raise my head and inhale. I wish I really were a fish in a pond, looking up at the world, limping towards Armageddon.

The phone rings and I only hear it dimly. The water—comatose effect is spreading fast and thick. I already do not belong here anymore.

*   *   *

The phone is still ringing thirty minutes later, when I am away from the tub and shivering. I cannot feel my hands on my face and my fingers are puckered. Gingerly, I plod across the room leaving puddles. There is a squelchy sound as my body rubs against the floor when I sit. Such indelicacy in bodily beauty.

I do not take the call. There is no malice in my conduct. It is self-explanatory disconnection. Roads cannot converge now. Roads have to diverge to be able to converge later, if people can only understand it. This is an intricate surgery which demands precision to be able to remove the tumour. The bile has to be mopped. This mop here has ugly jutting bristles.

The ringing stops and starts again five minutes later. I let my body loose on the floor. Sometimes, I hate the roundness of it. I wish I was more angular with the right kind of softness. I want it even though beauty is nothing but withering flesh. I want it, even though you will never caress it again. It looks like, we are born for this one devastating purpose: to suffer.

As the ringing stops, I wonder if it was the stranger who hounded me for a while. Has he found a new rodent to test his stalking skills on? The encounter gave me fleeting uncharted excitement and has left queasy memories. Looking forward to bouts of horror must be better than looking forward to nothing. Even if it is a case of self-inflicted Siberia.

History says, days of an anvil eventually come to an end. I resolve to be a good hammer, one that will pound well. One that you can be proud of.

*　　*　　*

I feed on a bowl of yoghurt and watch the news. The moving pictures re-tell old run-down yarns. Yesterday is today and tomorrow. Today is yesterday. Tomorrow is today. News is not new.

We are trying to draw a perfect picture by digging terribly dark holes. Not windows, but holes.

"I hope you run fast enough", I tell the television.

Funny Madness

I have a list of possibilities that which might happen if I ever see you inadvertently.

a. I force-feed you and kill you.

b. I freak out and bite your neck.

c. I dive into the nearest water body and drown (This is ridiculous, I know how to swim).

d. I (conveniently) faint and do not have to deal with the situation at all.

e. I gouge your eyes out and go mad with happiness.

f. I weep till you feel pity and take me in your arms.

g. I push you in front of a running truck and scream 'Accident!'

h. I follow you secretly to your home and murder you.

i. I hit you with a rod, you lose memory from concussion and I take care of you for the rest of your life.

Whatever happened to sanity, I do not know. What is sane, anyway? The state of mind, that never is. The kind of people/object they never are. That is what it is. The never-there. Sanity was born in a box and died in that box. The box did not open or break. It stays as a concept to separate between a man wearing a suit and a naked man taking a leak openly on the street, brandishing his penis to the passersby.

A mosquito hovers and finally settles on the bend of my knee. Mosquitoes are like thoughts, there is never killing enough of them. One dies, another sprouts. A million remains after a million has been killed. They will breed like dandelions mating to produce more dandelions.

What are we? We are not animals, certainly. Not just animals. We can make drug at home, with our hands. We did, while we were inside each other. The drug was all over the place, we crawled on fours and licked it with our tongues from the floor.

I am trying to tell you that I love you without having to be a poet. You will never understand my poetry.

*   *   *

The piece of paper looks very simple, with straight lines running across it. It came in a milky white envelope, the normal kind one sees everywhere. My name is written on it in small handwriting in dark blue ink. The handwriting is decidedly not yours but it is very very familiar. The paper has no smell and looks very new. It is written:

'You prefer to write, don't you? Let's write. I am right here.'

Why am I receiving such unhinged letters at 26? Where were these people in my childhood when I was a scrawny little kid? The note is without a sender's name but with an address. But I do not want to know who he is. I like him being without a face. I don't want to find him or identify him. These days, I am happier with strangers. I can make him look the way I want, I can make him have a beaked nose with an unruly mop of hair. Today, I do not feel scared of him at all.

I write:

> 'I just lost my home and I am
> waiting for my exit. Who are you,
> why should I write to you and why
> are you even there?'

I seal it in an old brown envelope which has no gloss of novelty. I am encouraging this man to write to me who might as well be a convict. The hopelessness of my situation has made me defiant? I am defying rules that which are practiced to keep ourselves safe. But I need to see this man who most persistently wants to be the aid, believes himself to be the aid. I want to see what he sees. If it is hypothetical, we will find out. If it is hypothetical, I will break it.

At times, this does seem like a fantasy life, with nothing and everything overlapping. Fullness and emptiness in seconds.

*   *   *

For the sake of the idea of sanity, I doodle this:

j. I pretend not to see you and walk past.

This can be wishful thinking. This can be a lie hoping to be true. This can be a lie which will stay a lie. No one can stop me for trying to cure madness with reassuring falsehood.

*   *   *

Unveil

gly can be beautiful. But ugly is ugly too. Ugly can be vicious, just the way it is supposed to be. I am trying to discover answers. But they are always changing. When I arrive how will they be? Pretty answers in laces? Unkind contorted answers shaped like pretzels?

I once had a friend in high school who behaved like a boy, wore lipstick and chased little stray dogs. She was blessed with nonchalance like none other. Always hiccupping loudly, chewing gums and sticking them under the desks were her forte. She loved to speculate and considered Jim Morrison to be some kind of a God, which was fair enough.

'He is a poet!' she used to hiss

She was never seen under the weather and her cult followers considered her to be an easy achiever. Someone with her tenacity had to win. I could understand that.

What I could not understand was how she deceived us all. On a Monday morning, the first day of the week of school, we came to know that her bloated body was recovered from the lake adjoining her house. That it was suicide because a note was found in her drawers. What hurt, was more than her death. It was the mangling of the legend. That she pretended to be our hero. That one can never know.

According to the reports, no reasons were found as to why she did what she did. She looked happy, her family said, even though the mother fainted every time there were too many questions; I still remember the tail of her orange saree flapping in the wind as everybody rushed to hold her. Even my mother, in all her quietness, cried that night, shaky simmering sobs that made the bed tremble. Father slept alone that night, his face set in stone, while my mother cradled me with an intensity that was almost frightful. Her vulnerable world was suddenly lit with the reality that children die, really young children die; more precisely really young children chose to kill themselves for no reason. That parents are not the ultimate shields, there is nothing darker than the terrible darkness within. But for that night, she felt she could protect me from myself, by almost barricading me with her own body. She had hiked up her nightie above her knees and fastened her legs around me, the fleshy manacles of the night. My father, for once, did not intervene with his patronizing counselling, he let his wife be. I could swear he was daunted by my mother's unexpected fit. He gargled less loudly that night, made no noise with his rubber slippers, and even washed the *thala* and glass all by himself. In our patriarchal household, men never did women's work and for once, he broke the rule, unasked. For that matter, he would have done anything she would have asked him to do that night. Her love was agonizingly chilling.

There is no preparation for what it is to come. Forewarnings do not help. Nothing helps, save the capacity to restrain, to not let go, to stand still and be hopeful. But everyone wants to let go. They cannot stand pregnant snail-walking, they demand fast and furious remedies. They want stardom waiting or they jump the train. In a way one has to love these people, they know what they want.

Now, I fall under the category of those who hate to wait but are too unwilling to die. This is the worst kind.

*   *   *

This is a long first letter. There is so much one can say. There is so much one can want to say to me. I never knew that my life would somersault and I would be reading a (any) letter of a really atypical man.

It reads:

> 'I am here because this is where I
> should be. This is my place, I have
> to be here. I am not here to give
> you pain. Believe it, if you can
> afford to. I am doing this because
> this is how things are meant to
> happen, I am sorry I cannot explain
> any better. Have you ever felt this
> way? Compulsion without a name.

This is premeditated. There is no coincidence. Why,
is a good question. Why should you have any part
in this at all? You should not. I cannot construct
suitable reasons. I will answer all your questions,
if you need to ask me. This is also not to establish
any relationship. This is selfless and it must sound
funny. This is without every transparent/translucent
agendas, whatever this is.

How I ever saw you? It is a story of 8 months
ago. You were in a black dress, alone and toying
with a book in your hand. And suddenly you break
into tears. The most un-self-conscious weeping. Do
you remember this evening? I stood in a corner and
stared and eventually followed you home. I know it
was improper, but back then I was not thinking. I
could not ignore the force. I wanted the force and I
did what it told me to. I saw you three more times
in the same week.

I will not ask you of your pain, your home or your need for an exit. I am not curious. You telling me anything or everything are on you. I am apologetic about my former obscurity but please understand that I was/am still without any formal clean definition.

I will wait when you will choose not to speak.

I am waiting till you write to me.

*   *   *

A chance encounter 8 months ago and a man followed me. How could I never know? If I take him literally, then he is a good man but goodness is a fairy tale in itself. It is funny he saw me when he saw me. That was the first night when I was starting to feel the devastation. When I started to see the irreparable damages crawling out of the crevices, crawling back to where they belong. It has been 8 months. It has been long and never short, and consistently pale.

Someone, who was not supposed to, has seen me grieving. It is not an embarrassment.

*   *   *

Unveil (Part 2)

These are large white sheets of paper, with light purple rim. I buy them immediately. They look so incredible that they can be stared at. Such purity one will not find on faces these days.

Outside, the Sun is melting. The warm yellowness feels like rain pattering against cheek. I sip the green apple slush which travels down my throat and seems to be creating a cold lagoon at the base of my stomach. If one has the humour, life is a theatre. With bad actors and good actors. Good actors remember their lines and dupe everyone. Bad actors forget the act and get duped. You cannot blame the good actors, but you must pity the bad ones. We do what we do because we forget about the aftermaths.

That they exist. That they will always exist even if we want to forget about them. That aftermaths are usually unpleasant.

Just outside the stationary shop, I see a relatively older man with a younger girl, the two of them deep into a love struck conversation. I instantly imagine that the man has a wife at home, a dog and two kids. The wife is a typical wife, uninteresting, haggard and certainly without any element of thrill. The man seeks excitement elsewhere and here he is, with youth promising him lost mirth. To avoid sounding like a feminist (even in imagination), I will assume the wife likes another man too, who makes her feel different. Who does not care for her scars, or the wrinkles under her eyes and kisses her with a fervour which only new love promises. However, this brings me to a question, a fanged question. A question very certain of itself.

What is oldness or newness really? When one lover seeks a new lover, the new lover is often someone else's old lover. So, basically there is no infidelity, but just worn perspectives. In this era of wear and tear, forever has to flee.

*   *   *

There was a reason to why we entangled; to never disentangle. To be tied with ropes of infinity. But reasons are like sparrows, always flying away.

*   *   *

The room is unusually dark as I enter. The darkness of an afternoon is eerie. I feel the walls staring at me with round eyes of an owl. They can even hoot. And the way they stare. Like, they can see things in me that I cannot. Like I am an alien invading their space. Only the newly bought sheets do not stare. They have not grown old enough to learn how to be patronizing.

My thighs feel tired and that reminds me of your nimble fingers running over them. For the briefest moment, I cannot remember your face. My heart seems to be straining against the rib cage. I cannot forget you yet. Forgetting cannot start so soon. I must remember, every sigh, every glance, every detail of how your pillow smelt. How all our firsts were. And seconds and thirds and lasts.

Also, I cannot believe that I want to retain your memory. That I do not want them to be washed away, the next time I shower. That may be I want to rewind and play you over and over again, like a video, after I insert a CD. The CD will be called 'The beautiful life of the man who was never there'. Or may be, 'The recordings of the invisible woman who watched'.

Wound, I will carry you. Gently. Or coarsely. But I will carry you. We will walk miles together. I might never sew you but I will touch and remember how much it bled.

*   *   *

It is starting to bother me that I cannot read a book. To be able to read seems like an act which was possible due to an organ that has been surgically removed from my body. I start with a book and desert it after a maximum of five pages. The unrest of the unread words is a tempest, mammoth in proportions. They cannot handle desertion or I cannot handle deserting them. I need them to keep telling me that the other world exists. What am I without the possibility of phantasy?

We always live for the greater life we are yet to have, the full glass we imagine having at the base of our mouth.

But, right now I am far away from the glass. In fact, I am nowhere near to a container that even faintly resembles the glass. I am coated with a syrupy film which acts as a world-screen and rescues me from human hymenopterans. This is all I have now.

*   *   *

'We can start with surrendering masks and pretensions. I do not want to sink further into the abyss of ambiguity. I want to sift clean words out of every tangled waste and recover only the legible. I want to be able to see my hands and ears, with their bumps and pores, just as they are.

I have not been expecting you when you arrived. I must tell you that I still buy insincere tears, which I find honest, even if they are not. I keep feeling like a bucket with a leakage, water slowly sipping out. The taps keep refilling me, now and then, but I also keep losing older water and there comes a time when I am totally filled with new water, with all older water gone. And that is a dreadful moment, when you do not know what you are containing.

I bought the perfect apartment (the one I could afford) and the perfect car (the one I could buy without having to pawn anything) and led a perfectly imperfect life for a long while, without knowing of course. I lived the great perfect nothing. And then someone was kind (unkind?) enough to shove me out of it and I must tell you that it takes long to wake up, even from a dead dream. But pain has its merits. My shoulders are not perched up anymore and I have stopped having wings. I walk on foot and the ground always feels hard.

It is funny to see that all the perfectness I thought I had were nothing but compromised decisions. Constrained and restrained and never exactly what I wanted. But I thrived in that deficiency happily. Ignorance is not over-rated.

My first letter to you. (Who are you?)

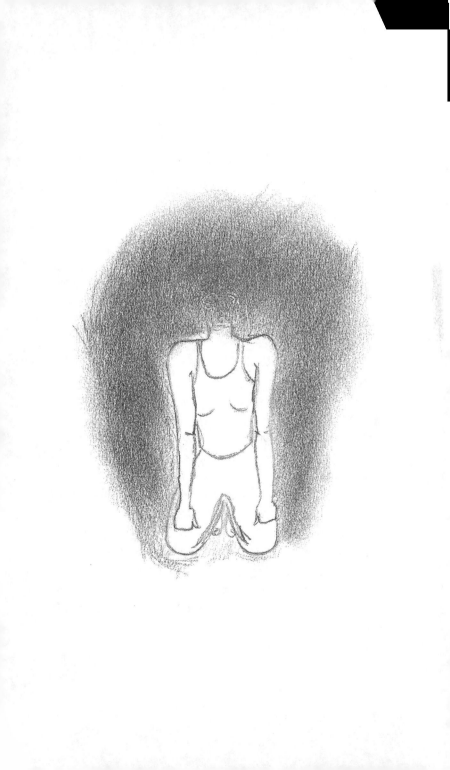

(Para)Normal

reakdown

Something is happening to me today. Almost paranormal. Something is closing in, comprehension, supernatural clarity. There might be a man in the mirror, performing Lobotomy on me, removing viscous nerve tracts, presenting me with palpable cognitive declarations. It is not changing my character, it can be equated with a sort of brain Cataract removal. May be he is saying *'One more minute, and it will be a different world again. The one you used to know'* .

May be I am saying 'You are like this scientist I used to know'

*   *   *

Let's begin with what I notice first. A lot of
clothes in the closet, not mine, lacy clothes with
hints of perfume, fading warmth of being worn with
love a long long time ago. I do not wear these kinds
of clothes, but I feel like I know them like I have
worn them myself. Delectable intimacy like I have
chewed on them, like meat. Known them as closely as
my face, rubbed them against my cheek, folded it,
seen it sit on skin, leave marks, tighten around
fat. But I cannot place them, I cannot historically
signify them. I am in that room, and the memory is
so snug to my conscience, that there is no line of
sight.

*   *   *

Next, I don't see T anywhere. Today is her birthday
and she was supposed to be here, all day. It smells
of honey, vanilla; my fingers sticky with floury
domesticity. Where is she? Ever had that dream where
you are naked, exposed to fully clothed strangers,
and you try to crumple your body to lessen the
obvious nakedness to the eyes that are not supposed
to see? I feel strangely bare, and the walls stare
back with hundred eyes or more; strong, piercing,
incising through my skin, the long of the neck, over
the bridge of the nose, down my scalp, still down my
back. Hundred truths hurling themselves at me. They
had been nesting inside the cracks all this time,
resolute at self-preservation.

The oven is set at 180 degree Celsius; it is dutifully helping in the making of a happy cake, soft and gooey at the centre, plump and typical.

*   *   *

I sit quietly on the chair. Inhale and exhale. My chest is about to crack revealing a dark, disgruntled heart. My whole body is decomposing. The fog of the coldest chill occupies the back of my neck and it's spreading, limb to limb, smoking everything in its course, a wild fire. There are images in my head, Godless images, unscrupulous, as brazen as death. As I perspire and feel this wicked mix of paralysis and absolute fright take over my body, the images get clearer. Like cold stale milk it drips all over my frontal lobe, blankets it enough that it becomes the only picture.

Wild wind must be howling outside, *kalbaishaakhi* at such an ungodly month. Trees must be shaking, leaves turning black, quivering like lips. I am sitting there at the base of the tree, looking up at the blitzkrieg that is tearing the dome apart. Infinite in this despair, I have to open my eyes. Everywhere I look is luminous with the secret I repressed. It is etched now on people's faces, on their hands, their dark hair. It has escaped from the cages of my conscience and spread like a virus. A story-telling virus that lets people know everything and in their knowledge, I become naked.

'I told you it will be a different world soon, the world you left behind' the scientist says

'Is this how you cure me?'

The scientist smiles and packs his instruments.

'You know we cannot be cured. We are incurably human and fashionably forgetful. It is time you remember to forget. "

Curtain Call

Denial

No. I will draw circles, circles within circles. I will eat little lumps of stone, build a crooked random kingdom and live in it with the population, not pretend to be a Queen. I will be hoarse, loud and unwrapped, ordinary person living within the concentric circles, invisible, visible only when I am inebriated, paint it yellow and unrecognizable, I will be the colour for a brief moment and then morph into a whore for men. It is all about penal satiation, there is no rush, no gun wounds. I will love too much and then not at all. Vagueness is the reality, vagueness is our name, vagueness is out of where we are born; there is no clarity in what we have spoken, felt, touched, nurtured. There is only estimation of what might have happened, a life we might have lived, an ugly carnival we might have bred, with cannibals, reptiles and jesters.

In all the lucidity of elusion, I have been a happy animal, lauding the brilliance of the blinding light, I was in control. I could control my death. I slowed everything down, I thought detonation under water must be softer, my edible cadaver will be delightfully tender pink for the spoons, knives and forks. That is what I became after all, a lover's fate, a lover's luscious tomorrow, a lover's sweet funeral.

But throughout, it remained a constant play. I loved you with an unclear velocity, and when it was over, I mixed images, I littered the pieces of our story and created fiction out of it. When I was finished, I did not remember you, and I was telling the world a history with no historical accuracy. I shamelessly retreated into the voluminous paranoiac religion of my own. In this world, every word uttered was faux, but without deliberation. You have to believe me that I did not know that I had created this counterfeit setting where I gave you a part to play with other synthetic players. All of you looked so *real*.

Can someone wake up one day to realize, with bursts of sadistic sanity, that the life led unwittingly for the past several months has been nothing but a dystopian, cleverly orchestrated drama that unfortunately, despite its grand tendencies, did not surpass the wretchedness of the facts it tried to escape from?

I have, right now.

Grief, o sombre grief, where did you take me? How could you leave me unbuttoned in winter? How did this happen? How could I have done everything but confront this one truth of my life?

*   *   *

How it started

For as long as I remember, I loved you. When we trotted in little dresses, our knees small and dirty, I held your hand and you slapped your wave of hair against my face, it was always too close to you. It would burn my face every time, the sting of the hairy cascade, black, alive, bobbing like the sea.

You held my hand till it got sticky and then left it, as quickly. I ran after you, offering you my orange popsicle; you took it and then wrenched my hand behind my back, and said *"Haath dhorish na amar"* (Don' t hold my hand). You crushed dry petals in your palms, your small porcelain palms, and it felt like my heart, a small artichoke heart would just burst inside my chest, and I would disgorge those brown veined petals right out of my mouth. But none of that happened, while I kept feeling that it would every afternoon.

We grew, slowly at first and then suddenly your body attained this strange vivaciousness; it was ripe, trembling and ready to melt in my mouth. And others'. The lady with the ring of fire in her loins. I saw so many men live fearlessly and die in that terribly incoherent fire. You laughed, you always laughed.

"Look at them fools, rotten to the core, trying to steal my vaginal fruit"

Saying that, you spread your legs, deliberately grossly apart, revealing your musky hairy triangle. I would crawl towards it, your firefly, and bury my head deep into that wet darkness.

"You will suffer for me, won't you? Suffer terribly?"

'Yes, yes yes'

I knew you were perhaps dysfunctional in a certain way, it was evident in the way you liked to see people suffer. You wanted to dismember all of them, tear them apart nimbly, without hostility, just a moist smoothness of a necessary action. As the longest surviving lover, you let me live. You waited for me to destroy myself but I had the imperishable hope that one day I would own you, put you on a leash, strip you and love you. I think maybe you wanted to be saved as well. Or not.

Sometimes, you sent me snapshots of you engaged in passionate coitus; each time a different man, progressively vulgar, your plump lips apart in some kind of a frozen supernatural thrill, you eyes always looking at the lens, at me, toying with my same, larger artichoke heart. The terribly expensive looking lingerie that you always wore in the pictures, were none of the kinds I had ever seen or worn or held. With me, you did not care for the fancy, I was an inferior mongrel, lapping up your dirt, your beauty, your sycophantic life, I had no life of my own.

I let you do what you wanted, and cried at my own contemporary disease. We were born in a society of monogamous love and polygamous secrets. When I cried, sometimes you cried with me, and together we mourned your disintegration, your chaos supernova.

Your body, already victorious of a million orgasms, would hold mine and croon old songs of our childhood. Silly ones, which had no resemblance to our malady.

'Ei poth jodi na shesh hoi, tobe kemon hoto tumi bolo toh?

Jodi prithibi ta shopner desh hoi, tobe kemon hoto tumi bolo toh?'

I heard you sing, and pretended I were in a different place, somewhere swollen with sea, our bodies glowing like phosphorus in marshes, scented and larger than ourselves. You would be a simpleton, loving rose shrubs, or maybe even *Gaanda,* wear ordinary white brassieres where the nipples would visibly strain against, tie your hair in an uncomplicated knot, lacquer it with warm coconut oil every Sunday. We would go on

short vacations, stay holed up in inexpensive rooms and express love freely; you would cup my breasts in your palms, wrap your body with mine and it would be a freefall.

"We can be happy together, please let us be"

The moment I said this, or other alternatives of this feeling, your body recoiled, went instantly cold, hard, like a forgotten wooden log out in the desert, untouched.

"Uncouth villager, fucking uncouth villager. What is it with you and happy endings, WHAT IS IT?"

With your sublimity sucked out of you in seconds, I became the mutt again, unpopular, unknown, famished like a beggar, on my knees, gyrating on the street, licking my own wounds. Expiry is not as easy as some would like to think.

*   *   *

Approximately 27 years after I had known, loved, and decapitated my senses, I met a man, wonderful enough to love me proudly. So much so that I did not understand. I had been bereft of receiving

love for long enough to have gathered that I would
never get any. When I experienced his love for the
first time, for a moment, I think I forgot I loved
you. I escaped into the deepest terrain, the broken
face in the mirror learned to speak the first few
words. He overlooked the gaping hole in my chest,
my excusable career, my lack of fashion, my stringy
hair; not that he wanted to build me, he simply
seemed fulfilled to be with such a non-descript
person. To add to the amusement, he found me exotic,
unreadable and hard shelled. I guess being with you
earned me an unbeatable shield. He loved scratching
on it, picking on parts of it with his nails and
unearth. While I laid at this lap of luxury, I was
catatonically petrified. Being bound and gagged by
an abominable loyalty, even in the realm of a man,
I only belonged to the elastic band of masochism. I
could no longer distil love as a clear solution; it
was eternally blighted by the beautiful mould.

*'WHAT? A man? You want a man invading your
body? You want a man looking at your skin, your
mounds, your genital? Is this what you want now?*

You screamed and scratched my face, nails with
your faces on them. You charged me like an unfed
bull determined to crush the Matador. Foaming at the
mouth, your beauty cracked up like a half done cake.
While I defended my body feebly, letting you hurt
my bony cage, the only one that was left to hurt,
I was swamped in a vibrant torpor. It was difficult
to feel any pain as my flesh wriggled, squirmed and
possibly cried in flesh language. I was thinking

that maybe for the first time, I was witnessing your love. It reduced you to the child you were, the one I knew. You were so severely famished, like our villagers, and so vain. So vain that you had to impose violence on me, you wished to gouge my eyes out before you were revealed. You tore my clothes, but I knew you were not looking at me sexually. Your glazed eyes had the hapless sweetness of extreme tear.

'You love me, don't you?'

Your ego came rushing back, back into your iris, making them darker and you slapped me, the hardest you could, with all of your body's defiance and your own sense of exclusivity. It was a vigorous slap, unsuitable for my unprepared face, full palmed.

'I am tired of your pettiness, you are so meagre that I want you to disappear. You are a weight on me, with your medieval desires. I don't love you, I loathe you, I pity you at best. I always have. Who else would have you?'

A small pool of blood lurked in my mouth and I felt a very unfamiliar feeling; anger. The leverage of love provided by a man. I knew in that moment, how empowered you must have been all this time. Your wings of steel were not your own, but of so many others'.

Did you know that you had been flying with borrowed appendages? The secret of my dragon queen was not her own after all.

Anger usually is a diverse feeling. It quickly multiplies and brings out its frenzied family. My anger generated an immodest family member, the magnificent streak of vengeance. I held back my feeling to spit at you, and instead of mucus, I spat words:

'I have someone. Who will have you now?'

You became a ghost for a second, your perfect oval face scrunched; your pores gave out a stench, a stench I had given off many a times when I felt I lost you. The animal fear. Your body trembled lightly, like a leaf in autumn, before it is about to begin its greatest fall. Before it learns to leave the higher abode, its blue proximity to the sky, starts to live among feet, trampling and disoriented, eventually floating under one such that did not go around it or walked on a different street or cared to consider about the life and breath of a golden leaf. It could be a man's, a woman's, a child's. The death of the leaf will be a moment's crunch, a fleeting relationship between the flat of the foot and an unaware leaf. You looked like that; I could see that in a moment, your face could be devoid of any beauty. It completely lacked the blood that should be pumping through the veins and giving you a flush. You were faceless, white tinged with light blue, a tossed canvas.

You fell over a chair and laid on the ground, murmuring. I could hear 'Mea Culpa' repeated over and over again. I loathed you for your fancy verbose melodrama even in that period of distress. I hated your sophisticated agony. Agony is naked, naked, naked. Agony is not clothed in couture.

Your murmurs stopped after a while; none of us moved. Your stillness did not deceive me; I could see your haunted mind leaping from corner to corner, aghast at my first declaration of imminent betrayal. Your stillness was not still. You were running amok, unboxed, untied, demanding my retraction in silent hushes. I could still read your mind, even in this salient moment of our disunion. Light turned to darkness, and we still laid there, you on the floor, I on another part of the floor, both of us sprawling in an unknown dimension, our feelings swapped for the first time. I tried to look at you, but all I could see was a part of your upturned foot; I did not try to get up and see your face. I had your face in my head, dust that never settles.

In that absolute silence, I hallucinated constantly; I saw you ripping my perfect man to shreds, a literal dream, your canines shining like piping hot razors. In the second, you were cooking for me with my mother. While you did't say anything, my mother in all of her 90's antediluvian youth, kept staring at me without a smile. The kitchen smelled of cardamom, and as the vegetables rustled in the *kodhai,* mother took the *khunti* out along with miniscule pieces of turmeric hued, salt and *moshla* drenched *alu* and *kumro*. She gestured me to taste and as I moved towards her, everything else disappeared. She clenched her hands and bellowed, 'Save the flower, not the fruit. Remember, please. Save the flower'.

In the third, we both were falling deep into an abyss, unafraid, falling without a sound. You did not look at me, but I tried to catch your arms. They bobbled a little out of reach, and I almost sabotaged the fall by trying to come too close to you. Your arms turned infinitely long and tentacle-like, defying human diameters, closing in on me in an eternal embrace. While life escaped through my mouth, a vapour like release, I realized that all you have become is this one embrace, without identity; this interlocking death is what you gave me, the last and only act of fondness.

*   *   *

When I woke up with a start, it was morning. Bright, gay yellow light scorning dark corners. My mouth was parched and yesterday's euphoria had gone amiss. The perfect day for living, not pretension. My body ached from being awkwardly juxtaposed, just like my mind. As last night's memory came flooding back, my heart leapt at the thought of you. Ironically I felt no love for him, all was gone, in the course of the night, like I held his love for all this time, just to tell you and revel in your anguish. Like it was not love at all, he did not exist in my future. I ensnared myself believably so I could ensnare you.

This self inflicted ambush had a very short life span.

I scrambled onto my feet, unsure of everything again. Unsure of the damages, of what I had split open and could sew back. Even in pain, my old life had a rhythm, a masochistic pattern I had been following for ages. I was bound, gagged, killed enough times to idolize my perpetrator as my God. Psychiatrists might label it as Stockholm syndrome. But being on this side, I could say it was a form of undiluted love. Not everything is born out of purity, absolute white. Filth is a great mother. Filth sometimes lets you scoop yourself out and attain a puritan ability to perceive objects without the magnificent taint they are born/live with. It can be a curse too, for some things deserve to be seen as they are.

As I looked your way, you seemed to be positioned the same like you were last night. You had not left. My whole body jostled with unexpected hope and I knew I could not live with a man, any man, him, anybody other than you. The love I had for you is the kind that makes young women kill themselves in anonymous cheap motel rooms, drowned or wrists slashed, water or blood, a blue body or a red one, a violent end to together, forever. I could be one of those girls, fortunate to be taking my own life, a sensational purposeful death rather than a decaying obscure one.

Your hair covered half of your face, your eyes veiled and your thin long arms by your side. Chaos had left you and your hair sparkled against the sunniness that the window let in. You were a vision and I stared and I knew I would do anything to have you take me back, as any chosen component in your life; arrogate, quench, thrill, wring out my plain life. Yesterday was a brave day, an unanticipated leap, a blind stab, an aberration.

'Wake up'

My voice was tiny, hoarse; I was scared to touch you, of your catastrophic wrath. But I needed to hear the fire in your voice, even if it meant I burnt. I bent down and removed the few strands of hair.

'Wake up'

My voice was thin, unlike myself, as if in fear I took on someone else's voice. I might as well could have gone to a voice bank, and selected a high pitched quavering voice and said, 'Yes, I will take this. This sounds like my fear. This dignifies it perfectly'. And a rabbit would have handed over a small, inconspicuous vial with a clear liquid. One gulp, and I would be a customized buyer braving my brand new fear.

'Wake up'

*   *   *

One can never understand a few things. Èven simple things. Even simple everyday realities. When we cannot process an event, we never get over it; it is beyond denial. Denial is understanding without acceptance. It is different and possibly less complex. When someone claims to not understand a socially accepted simple occurrence, it can seem to be a kind of retardation.

*   *   *

It was told to me that I (possibly) held your body throughout that day and the next till your neighbour (possibly somebody you had slept with; a married man with three kids) came banging on your window, the same window which let the Sun in and made your hair shine like precious black gold. In his words, your body was 'wilting with a terrible stench' while I cradled you. Aghast, when he questioned me, I had answered that I was trying to 'wake you up'.

Cause of death was a massive heart failure. You were thirty two years old.

Time of death, 1.51 am.

It was told to me while you were being incinerated that I asked 'I don't understand why you are burning me' while my mother cried inconsolably. She said she moved in with me because I had a 'nervous breakdown' but I do not remember seeing her around me. She also told me that sometimes I posted letters to myself and described them as 'means to the light' .

I did see you, till this time. Till this time, eight months later, I thought you were alive. This makes everything I thought, told, felt—fascinating fiction. I garbled every detail except the core.

Confirmations

1. The letters neatly stacked, in my own handwriting.

2. No cigarette smoke, stumps, ash, remnants. Your smokiness nowhere.

3. Your death certificate

4. The picture of the man who I tried to leave you for, for a night. Mother said I did not recognize him when he came to see me.
5. Your clothes in my wardrobe that I insisted came with me. Blouses, dresses, lingerie.

*   *   *

There can never be an end to this. Your voice is like the sea, washing me, filling the gaps between my toes with froth every time.

Epitaph on the wall

One day,
Alice stepped out,
to douse the foolish smoke, its
gangrenous arms,
were reaching too far into her kitchen.

When she unexpectedly fell into the hole,
which she did not know was of a rabbit' s,
she was glad it was a spiralling hole, and not a
box.

Acknowledgements

To,

Jonas, you will never know how much . . .

My mother, for seeing me through sanity and insanity. My father, for being insane enough to understand insanity.

My rocks, Vivek and Trina; the best people in the world who love me unflinchingly. Special thanks to Vivek for his contribution with the illustrations.

Dheeman, for being able to recognize the little things. If nothing else, we will always have our tree. And thank you, for gluing those scraps of paper back to life.

Those infinite people who visited and strayed. Visited and stayed, to you . . . K, D, A, S, S.

My fish, Ciara and Corsica, who only needed a watery orb to be happy.

My dog, who I never had.

All my demons, underneath my bed; they inspire.

and,

The man, in the white.